Disney's
SMALL WORLD LIBRARY
DONALD AND THE BIG CHEESE
An Adventure in The Netherlands

GROLIER ENTERPRISES INC.
DANBURY, CONNECTICUT

Printed in the United States of America.
Developed by The Walt Disney Company in conjunction with Nancy Hall, Inc.
ISBN 0-7172-8210-4

Daisy Duck waited anxiously for the president of the Duckburg Cheese Factory to open the judges' envelope. She looked at all the tables filled with fancy cheese dishes. There were omelettes, soufflés, pies, and cakes.

"The first prize in this contest is a free trip for two to the Netherlands, the place where they make more cheese than anywhere else in the world!" Daisy whispered to Donald under her breath.

Just then the president made his announcement. "And now, for the most imaginative cheese recipe, a windmill cheesecake, the winner is . . . Daisy Duck." The crowd of cheese lovers cheered.

"Daisy! You won!" cried Donald.

During the long plane ride, Daisy and Donald thought about all the wonderful things they could see and do in the Netherlands.

When they arrived in Amsterdam, the capital of the Netherlands, they were greeted by their very handsome tour guide, Hans. Daisy smiled at Hans. Hans smiled at Daisy as he took her hand. Donald just looked on. Maybe things weren't going to work out so well after all, he thought.

"We shall begin our tour with a boat ride around the beautiful city of Amsterdam," Hans said.

"That sounds lovely!" Daisy replied. And as they rode through the canals, Hans showed Daisy all the important sights. Donald sat and listened to what Hans had to say. He tried to think of something to tell Daisy that Hans didn't already know. Donald wished he had read his guidebook more carefully.

After the boat ride, Hans brought Daisy and Donald to a sidewalk café to try a favorite local snack, raw herring dipped in chopped onions. Daisy thought hers was delicious.

Donald didn't get a chance to find out what he thought of his.

On their way to one of the local museums, Hans took Daisy and Donald to a little shop where old-fashioned Dutch wooden shoes were still made.

"The shoemaker hollows out a block of wood," Hans explained, "then decorates the shoes with paint. Wooden shoes were designed to help farmers walk through their muddy fields. Most people in the Netherlands don't wear them much anymore. But they are really quite comfortable and practical for our damp weather."

Hans walked briskly around the shop in his wooden shoes, showing Daisy and Donald how comfortable they were. Then Hans helped Daisy try on a pair.

"Oh, I just love them!" Daisy exclaimed. "Donald, let's each buy a pair."

Donald chose a pair that was too small, and he couldn't get the shoes off once he put them on. Not wanting the others to notice, he decided he'd just wear them as best he could until he figured out how to get them off.

After leaving the shoe store, Hans, Daisy, and Donald walked to the Stedlijk Museum. There, Hans showed them the work of the famous Dutch painter Vincent van Gogh.

"Hans isn't the only one who knows something about art," Donald grumbled to himself. "I'll show him." Donald puffed up his chest and informed his companions that he knew valuable artwork when he saw it. "For example, take this lovely piece of modern sculpture," Donald began.

But before he could finish, a janitor came to empty the trash out of Donald's "sculpture." Donald saw Daisy giggle, but Hans turned away so Donald wouldn't see him laugh.

"How about going for a bicycle ride in the countryside?" Hans asked Donald and Daisy. "Bicycle riding is a favorite pastime in the Netherlands."

"What a wonderful idea, Hans," Daisy exclaimed. Donald thought for a moment. Donald could ride a bicycle—he could ride a bicycle very well! He'd show Daisy that even if he didn't know much about art, he could ride a bicycle better than Hans.

Soon the three were riding through the Dutch countryside, passing field after field of brightly colored tulips.

Hans, of course, was an excellent cyclist. He rode without touching the handlebars, and he gracefully scooped up a bunch of tulips for Daisy.

"Oh, Hans!" Daisy thanked him, blushing, holding the soft blooms up to her face.

"Oh, brother!" Donald muttered under his breath. Wasn't there anything this guy Hans didn't do well?

"That's not so hard," Donald thought. Then he bent over and tried to pick some more flowers for Daisy. And he almost did it, too, except his wooden shoes slipped off the pedals. Donald's bicycle went flying—and so did Hans and Daisy.

Daisy and Hans landed in a tangle of tulips and
bicycles, while Donald landed on a very surprised cow.
Timidly Donald held out his broken bouquet of tulips. But
Daisy was much too busy untangling herself from the
heap to notice Donald or his tulips.

"Perhaps we should take a break from riding for a
while, my friends," Hans suggested. "I see some wonderful
old windmills that are still in use. Let's go visit them."

Donald stomped off, well behind Daisy and Hans. Daisy seemed to have forgotten all about Donald. And he didn't like it—not one bit!

"This windmill pumps water off the land, and back to the sea," Hans explained. "Without dikes and pumps, nearly half of the Netherlands would be underwater."

"Isn't that amazing?" Daisy gasped.

But Donald wasn't listening. His feet and pride hurt too much. So he just sat down on the first thing he found and pretended not to care in the least.

Donald tried to figure out how to get Daisy's attention. He was so lost in thought that he didn't even notice when a vane of the windmill got stuck under his collar. Before he could even call out for help, it lifted him higher and higher up in the air. Then the windmill dumped him into the waterwheel, and Donald went sloshing down the canal.

"These waterwheels move water through the canals toward the next mill, which grinds wheat into wheatmeal," Hans continued to explain.

"Yes, I see," said Daisy, watching the waterway and nodding her head. Suddenly she noticed a familiar form falling into the waterway and heading toward a waterwheel. "Oh, my goodness, Hans, it's Donald!" Daisy said, pointing to the canal. "What is he doing?"

Wet and exhausted, Donald scrambled onto the bank of the canal.

"This is not the time or place to be taking a swim, Donald!" Daisy chided. "It's rude to go off like that—and you're missing what Hans has to say," she added in an angry whisper. Meanwhile, Hans explained how the wheatmeal ground in the mill was used to feed the many dairy cows raised throughout the country.

"I don't care about what Hans has to say!" Donald whispered back, just as angry as she. But Daisy was once again listening to Hans and didn't even hear.

"And I bet all those well-fed dairy cows are the reason why there is so much rich milk to make those delicious Edam and Gouda cheeses for which you Dutch are so famous," Daisy observed.

"Precisely!" Hans exclaimed, taking Daisy's hand and giving it a gentle pat. Daisy blushed.

This was too much for Donald to bear. He wasn't about to stand around and watch Hans hold Daisy's hand!

But suddenly Donald couldn't move. His tail feathers were stuck between the turning millstones, and no matter how hard he tugged, he couldn't get loose.

Donald was dragged past the pulley that lifted sacks of grain up to the top of the mill. One of the hooks caught Donald's shirt. He had no choice but to call for, of all things, Hans's help.

"Quick! We've got to save him," Hans called to Daisy as he raced up the windmill's winding stairs.

Daisy ran after Hans.

Hans grabbed a burlap sack and held it up to catch Donald just before he fell into the chute that led to the grindstones at the bottom of the mill.

"How could you be so careless?" Daisy scolded.

Donald couldn't reply. He knew he should be grateful to Hans for saving him, but he was too embarrassed to say a proper thank-you.

"It could happen to anyone, Daisy," Hans said gently. He was too polite to make Donald feel worse.

"I think we've had enough of windmills for the moment," Hans said briskly. "And I know just the place to visit next. There's a little delft pottery shop not too far from here. Then we can rest our tired feet—eh, Donald?" he added sympathetically.

Donald nodded his head weakly. He wasn't sure whether or not Hans was making fun of him. And his feet certainly were tired in the tight wooden shoes.

When they reached the shop, Donald's feet were really
aching. While Daisy bought a teapot, Donald tried to pull
off his wooden shoes. He gave one shoe a tremendous
yank. His elbow bumped into a large, expensive vase. It
teetered. It tottered. Then it fell off the shelf!

Before the vase hit the ground, Hans grabbed it. He
didn't laugh at Donald. Hans just put his fingers to his
lips and gave Donald a friendly wink. And he didn't tell
Daisy what had happened. Donald began to wonder about
Hans. Maybe he isn't so bad, Donald thought as he
decided to look for a better place to take off his other
shoe.

As they left the pottery shop, Hans announced he had a special surprise for Donald and Daisy. He took them to the town of Gouda, famous for its delicious cheese. They arrived, as Hans had planned, just in time for the cheese factory's 200-year anniversary celebration! Proudly Hans showed Donald and Daisy where and how the cheese was made.

"And now it's time for the party!" Hans told them both in an excited voice. Daisy clapped her hands in anticipation. Donald wasn't quite sure how to feel.

All the spectators cheered, especially when the proud cheese workers rolled out the world's largest wheel of Gouda cheese. But the wheel was so big that the workers couldn't hold on to the slippery wax coating. The giant cheese started to roll downhill.

Everyone ran to safety, except Daisy, who tripped on the rough pavement. She fell directly in the path of the giant cheese!

"Oh, no!" shouted Donald as the cheese rolled toward Daisy. He could see that Hans was much too far away to get to Daisy in time. But as Donald ran to help her, he stumbled and flew headlong into the wheel of cheese!

"Oh, Donald, you saved my life!" Daisy said gratefully, giving Donald a big kiss.

"Aw, it was nothing," Donald began. Then he realized that suddenly Daisy was once again paying attention to *him*.

But before he could say another word, Hans rushed over to them.

"How can we ever repay you for your bravery, Donald?" Hans asked.

"Well, there is one thing. . . . You can help me take off my other shoe," Donald blurted out. And everyone, including Donald, had to laugh.

Did You Know...?

Every country has many different customs and places that make it special. Some of the things that make the Netherlands special are mentioned below. Do you recognize any of them from the story?

Amsterdam is the capital of the Netherlands. It has more bridges than any other city in the world—550 bridges altogether. The bridges allow people to cross the city's many canals.

Vincent van Gogh is considered one of the Netherlands' greatest painters. But during his lifetime, he was considered a failure because he sold only one painting.

About half of all Dutch people own and ride bicycles. Many ride their bicycles to work instead of driving cars.

The Netherlands has 4 million dairy cows. They produce 20 billion pounds of milk a year. That's enough milk to fill a large lake.

Edam and Gouda cheeses are two of the most famous Dutch cheeses. Each cheese is named after the Dutch town where it was first made.

Long ago, windmills like this one were used
to grind wheat into flour. The Dutch
relied on the power of the wind to
turn the arms of the windmills.

Tulips are the national flower of the Netherlands. The
Dutch grow several thousand different kinds of tulips and
ship them all over the world.

Klompen (clom-pin) is the Dutch word for wooden shoes. Today they are mostly worn by gardeners, fishermen, and farmers at work.

This pretty blue-and-white patterned pottery that Daisy is admiring is delftware. It is named after the Dutch town of Delft, where it was first produced several centuries ago.